The Champlain MONSTER

Written and Illustrated by
Jeff Danziger

The
Champlain

MONSTER

Written and Illustrated by
Jeff Danziger

The New England Press
Shelburne, Vermont

For Matthew and Kim

For additional copies of this book or for a catalog of our
other titles, please write:

The New England Press
P.O. Box 575
Shelburne, VT 05482

Author's Note

A sincere note of thanks goes to the people who helped this book get written: Glenda Bissex, Pat Fair, Susan Weber, Steve Young, the editors and publishers of the *Times Argus* and the *Rutland Herald,* and most of all to the author's longsuffering and patient family, for whom the word monster has taken on a new meaning.

It should also be mentioned that all of the characters in this book are purely fictitious. Except, of course, the monster itself. After all, fiction can only be stretched so far.

If there's one thing I've learned, it's that you can't believe everything they tell you in school. Especially about how the world started. Most of it is just made up because nobody was there. Certainly none of my teachers was there. They just teach what they read in books. And the whole story is a lot more. Everything about the world isn't in books, that's for sure. Not even this book.

Most kids just sit in school and listen to the teacher go on about the dinosaurs and the triceratops and how they were all wiped out when the glaciers came crunching down during the ice age. And the next day they fill in the answer on a test, and the teacher marks it right, so they figure that's the way it happened.

I used to fill in all those answers too, and get hundreds on tests. But not any more. Not after last summer. Because I know that what they teach in school isn't always so. And if they were wrong about the dinosaurs, what else are they wrong about?

2

You might not believe me, because it is a little hard to swallow. But you can certainly believe Tracy.

Tracy is my sister, a year younger than I am. We get along pretty well for sister and brother. I think that's because Tracy is small and needs me to protect her. But there's another thing about Tracy that you have to know.

She is the smartest person I have ever met. She can memorize things by just reading them once. She can do math in her head as fast as a pocket calculator. Not only that, but she can play a violin, which is a very hard thing to do. You know when most little kids play the violin, it sounds like a frying cat, but when Tracy does it, it sounds like real music.

I like Tracy pretty well, but it's not easy having a really smart sister. I don't know whether I'm going to be able to stand it when she gets older. But for right now it's kind of helpful. Everything she reads goes right into her little computer brain. Then if you need some information anytime, you just ask. For instance, she knows all the rules to all card games, and all sports, and major league players, and she can't get lost because she knows the road maps all around here. And she knows all the presidents and the wars in American history. And she can check my math homework faster than the teacher can.

She can do really helpful things, too. One time

4

we had our canoe tied up on the lake, and the wind blew very hard during the night, and the next morning it was gone. Tracy figured out where the wind would have blown it down the lake, and we went there and sure enough, there it was waiting for us.

You have to respect brains like that.

Where we live is pretty far up north, right on the shores of Lake Champlain. The winters are long and cold. The wind comes down from Canada, swooping along the frozen lake and blasting everything in its way. For about five months everything is snow, and it's a battle to keep the house warm. We leave for school in the dark, and get back in the dark. Sometimes it gets super cold; the cars don't start, and the pipes freeze, and the buses don't run, and we get to stay home from school. Other times there are ice storms, the power lines snap, and we have to use candles and the wood cook stove.

But I don't mean to make winter sound like a bad time. Because there's plenty to do. There's

8

skating and skiing, of course, but there's also our own fun. We build snow castles and snow forts, gigantic ones. Last winter we built one just like Windsor Castle, which is where the Queen of England lives, or at least that's what Tracy says. She had read a book about it and knew exactly what it looked like.

And there's other things to do, like ice fishing. My father has a little shanty that he pulls out on the ice late in the winter when he's sure it is frozen thick enough. The shanty is on runners, and inside there's a stove and shelves and pots and pans, and a radio, and lights and books and a table and everything. There's a hole in the floor to fish through, but we make other holes outside as well.

My father lets us go out fishing with him, and sometimes he lets us go out alone. We start a fire in the stove and put bait on all the hooks. Then we wait for the tip-ups to snap which means there's a fish on the line.

Tracy doesn't like to take the fish off the hooks, so I have to do that. But she doesn't mind cleaning them once they're dead.

If you know anything about Lake Champlain you know that you can't see far down in the water. Tracy says that is because the lake is so large that it has tides just like the ocean, only not as high. The water moves back and forth, pulled by the gravity of the moon. The bottom of the lake, made of soft gray slate, is stirred up. So the water always has a cloudy gray color. It isn't dirty or anything, and it won't hurt you to drink it but it is impossible to see the bottom.

It's a nice size for a lake. It's big enough to be exciting, but small enough to see across. In late winter, when the ice is frozen very thick, you can even walk back and forth between Vermont and New York. On windy days, there are ice boat races.

Tracy says the ice is sometimes two feet thick. Even when there are huge cracks, and the ice makes snapping, crunching sounds, it is pretty safe. On sunny winter days my father takes us for walks out to the middle of the lake, and we have picnics there on the ice. In the summer, when the sun is hot and bright, we paddle out in the canoe and try to figure out where we had had the picnic on the ice.

CANADA

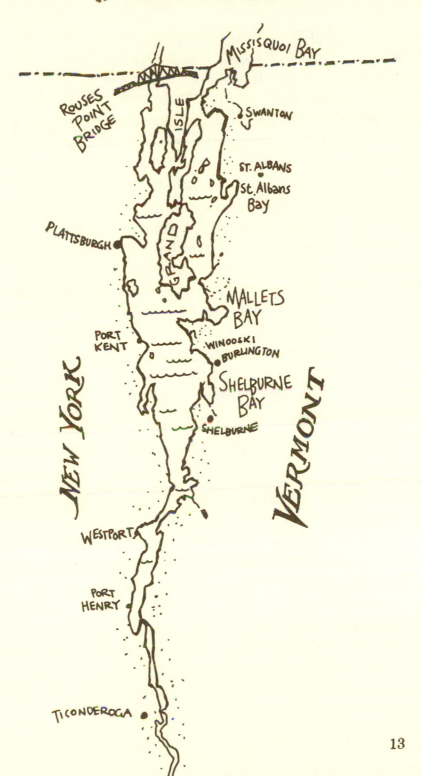

MISSISQUOI BAY

ROUSES POINT BRIDGE

ISLE

SWANTON

ST. ALBANS

St. Albans Bay

PLATTSBURGH

GRAND

MALLETS BAY

PORT KENT

WINOOSKI

BURLINGTON

SHELBURNE BAY

SHELBURNE

NEW YORK

VERMONT

WESTPORT

PORT HENRY

TICONDEROGA

13

The winter before last had been fine for ice fishing. There hadn't been much snow, but the weather had been very cold. One night the thermometer in our wood shed went down to fifty below zero. No kidding. In weather like that, you can hardly breathe outside. The ice on the lake cracks and crunches and even gets too cold for skating. At night the stars give enough light to see by even if there is no moon.

My father would get home from work as early as he could so we could go down to the lake to check our lines. There would usually be a fish on every tip-up, but sometimes the holes would be nearly frozen again. I would pull up the lines, and my father would run the ice auger down the holes again. Then we'd set the tip-ups again and head on back. By that time it would be completely dark.

On cold, cold nights the moon was bright silver, so bright it hurt to look at it, and the ice would glisten pure white. Our breath turned to white fog, and I could feel the air freezing the inside of my nose and throat. Cold like that can hurt and even kill, but those moonlit frozen nights were pretty in their own way. I used to try and remember what the lake was like in the middle of summer, when the water was blue and warm and the sun glinted from the waves. How could anything stay alive through the winter down in the black, icy water? Sometimes Tracy would tag along, but it was usually too cold for her.

One night, after two weeks of below zero cold, we came back from the lake with about thirty fish. My mother and Tracy cleaned them and wrapped most of them for the freezer. Tracy held one of the fish up and looked at it carefully.

"This isn't a fish, Eddie," she said to me.

And it wasn't. At first we didn't know what it was. It looked something like a fish scale, but it was much too big. In fact it was nearly as big as my hand, and sort of a greeny-brown color.

My father looked at it. At the end of the scale was a ridge of white skin that had torn loose from something.

"Probably a shingle off an old shanty that fell through the ice," he said, "but it doesn't look like wood exactly."

It looked like a fish scale.

"There's a whale down there," Mom said.

"Whales don't have scales," Tracy said.

"If this is off a fish, I'd like to land it," my father said, "He'd feed us for ten years."

"And we'd need a new freezer for sure," said my mother. Tracy quietly took the scale and put it in a plastic sandwich bag and put it in the freezer.

Every night from then on Tracy insisted on going with us in the evening to check the tip-ups. She always wanted to go out on the ice with my

father every week-end and holiday. She went around to the other shanties and talked to all the other ice fishermen. She never actually talked about the scale, but she asked the fishermen if they had pulled up anything strange recently. No one had anything like a scale.

But my father did. Over the next few weeks, he brought up five more of the strange scales. Some were larger than others and some were a darker green, but they were all the same shape and had the ridge of torn flesh along one end.

Tracy kept all the large scales in the freezer. One day she made me go with her out to the shanty of an old fisherman named Pete, whose shanty was off by itself. My father knew this man and sometimes stopped and talked. But Tracy and I had always been a little scared of him. His shanty was about as run-down as it could be, and my father said Pete even slept in it most of the

winter. He had a little kerosene stove in the shanty and some pots and pans and cans of food, but not much more. He was sitting out in front of the shanty in the bright sun squinting at us.

"Nice day for the beach, ain't it?" he said. His face was very red and wrinkled, but his smile was friendly enough.

"Did you ever catch anything like this on your hooks?" Tracy asked him. She held out a plastic bag with one of the scales in it.

The old man examined it carefully. He stopped smiling.

"Where'd you catch this?" he said at last.

"Back closer to shore. We've pulled up six of them this winter."

"Very strange," he said, holding the scale up to the sun. "About ten years ago I was living on the other side of the lake, and when I was fishing that winter, I pulled up some of these. No one knew what they were."

He paused and looked up at us.

"Then two years ago I was fishing further north on this side, and I pulled up the same thing."

"What do you think they are?" he asked Tracy.

Tracy didn't answer. So I asked him.

"We don't know. What do you think?"

"Well, when I pulled up the first ones, I thought they might be part of some sort of plant that grew on the bottom, that no one had ever seen. But it's not right for a plant. I figured that it had to be part of a very big fish."

"That's what I think, too," I said. "Did you ask anyone about it, a fish expert or anyone like that?"

"Well," he said, "I did ask some people I knew, but by that time the whole thing had sort of gone bad, since I didn't have a freezer to keep it in. I thought about it and decided that if I was ever going to have anybody give me more information I was going to have to get more evidence or they'd think I was just another crazy old fisherman. That summer I went back out in a boat and scouted all around the place I had fished the previous winter."

"What did you find?" I asked.

"Nothing," he said. "You know how this lake is. I couldn't see anything down through the water. I even fished around some with a deep-sea fishing hook. But there was nothing down there. Certainly not any big fishes."

"Then what do you think it was?" I asked.

"Well," he said, "I think . . . ah . . . I think there's someone calling you two back over there."

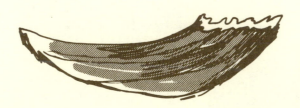

That night Tracy told me her idea.

"It's not a fish Eddie, not a big fish, not a fish at all. The scale is much different from a fish scale. It's longer and much thicker. And fish scales are sort of clear; this one is dark."

"And whatever it is has been alive for a longer time than a fish lives," I said. "If the old man said he pulled up some scales ten years ago, then whatever-it-is would be way over ten years old. More like twenty."

"It's a lot older than that," said Tracy, "an awful lot older."

"Maybe fifty years?" I said.

"Maybe fifty-thousand years," Tracy said.

"What?"

"Don't you see?" she said, all excited now. "Whatever is down there has been there a long, long time. Its scales haven't changed at all. It's been there since before there were even men in this part of the world. I don't know what it is, but it is sleeping through the winter. When it's awake in the warmer months, it never goes around where there are fishermen. But in the winter it sleeps, and that's when it gets snagged on fish hooks."

"You mean it's right under our fishing shanty?" I said. "It could destroy the whole thing."

"No, it can't," she said. "In the first place, it's asleep, and it can't wake up till the water gets warmer. And in the second place, it doesn't attack anything."

"How do you know?"

"Because if it were the type of animal to attack boats and fishing shanties, it would have done it long before this, and it would have been seen."

"And," I said, "we would have already heard about it in school."

For the rest of that winter we didn't do much more than think about the whatever-it-was sleeping under the ice. Tracy made me drill more holes with the auger farther out from our fishing shanty. At each one we dropped a line down to the bottom and tried to hook some more scales. Tracy kept a chart and measured the distance between the holes carefully.

Sometimes we got one of the scales and sometimes we didn't. By the end of the winter we had pulled up twenty-three scales. Tracy had them all arranged and numbered in separate plastic bags in the freezer. Her chart showed that the thing must be over sixty feet long.

"And that's only the part that we can reach," she pointed out to me and Pete. "There might be a lot more we can't reach with our lines."

By this time we had become pretty good friends with Pete. Pete kept our stuff out in his shanty, so it wouldn't clutter up my father's shanty. In fact we didn't tell my father and mother what we were doing. Parents are strange: They're always the first ones to believe that their children are crazy.

Tracy had read everything she could find on prehistoric creatures. She took out books from the school library, and after she had read all those, she made the librarian send away for more detailed books from the state library. Remember, I told you that Tracy remembers everything. Everything that goes into her head stays there. Nothing is forgotten.

Then one day when we were walking home from the school bus, we stopped and looked around. The snow was melting, the sun was warm again, and the road was getting mushy. There was no doubt about it: Winter was fading. Spring was on the way.

"When the lake water gets up to around 40 degrees," Tracy said, "I think it will come out of hibernation, and then we've got to be there."

"But by that time, the ice will be getting soft," I said, "and Pop will have moved the shanty back into shore."

"We'll have to go out on the ice and wait," she said.

"They'll never let us back out on the ice in spring." I said. "Besides, I'm not so sure I want to go out there then anyway."

"What?" She looked at me as if I had suggested something insane. "Don't you want to see what it is?"

"Not if it means falling through the ice. Look, Tracy, we don't even know if there really is anything out there. You don't know what it is. It might be very dangerous. It might be nothing. All we have is a bunch of old scales and a story from

an old man who has been fishing too long. You don't even know if there's anything down there."

"Of course there's something down there," she shouted at me, "and it's alive and it's sixty feet long, and it's coming out of hibernation when the water warms up."

"And what are you going to do?" I shouted back. "Stand there on the shore with a cup of coffee and a donut?"

"You're so stupid!" she yelled.

"And you think you know it all!" I bellowed.

"What are you two yelling about?" my mother said from the porch, where she was hanging up laundry in the warm sunshine.

"Nothing," I said, and Tracy stamped into the house.

Later that evening, I went into Tracy's room.

"Listen," I said, "I'll go out there with you, if you really want to. But I think we should tell Pop about your theory."

"No," she said, "nobody else. Just you and me, Eddie."

"Why?"

She thought for a while and finally said, "Because, Eddie, it's not a theory. It's really out

28

there. I know it. And second of all because it's been there for a long, long time."

"Well, what's wrong with telling someone older about it?"

"Because if anyone knew. . . "

"If anyone knew. . . what?"

"They'd probably try to kill it."

The weather grew warmer and warmer, and the days got longer. When we came home from school in the afternoon it would still be light. The ice on the lake started to break up, and the surface was mushy. Most of the ice fishermen already had brought their shanties in to shore for the warm months. Pete's shanty was still out there. My father said that if he didn't get it in soon, it would sink through the ice.

The more I began to think about Tracy's idea of the thing under the ice, the more worried I became. I really wanted to tell someone, but Tracy said I couldn't. She said people would think we were crazy. I knew people would think we were crazy, and I began to think that they might be right.

I had begun to work on our canoe, cleaning it up and patching the scratches. Tracy said we would need it. "Need it for what?" I thought as I scrubbed away at the bottom. But Tracy wouldn't give me any reasons. I began to think that she didn't trust me with any real important secrets, or maybe she didn't know herself and was just covering up.

When Spring comes up here, it sort of comes and doesn't come. It can be very warm one day, and the back roads turn to slush and mud and the maple sap begins to flow. The snow melts and our front yard turns into a muddy lake and my mother's daffodils start up through the muck. And our snow castles collapse and the snowmen fall over and everything is a mess. But it's a nice kind of mess because you know winter's over.

And then, just when you are sure that there is no more cold weather coming, it clouds over and freezes the mud solid and snows worse than before. Then it gets warm again, and then cold again, off and on for about a month.

My father had given us a small canoe to paddle around in near the shore. We had gotten pretty good at it, but we never went any distance out in the lake. The canoe was a nice size, but it was too small to take out in the choppy waves in the center. And if the wind came up strong, we

couldn't paddle hard enough to go against it. But on a sunny summer day, when the water was calm, there was no nicer way to spend time, paddling along the shore, fishing and talking and exploring.

I took the canoe off the rack in the garage and put it across two carpenter's horses in the yard. I washed out the inside and fixed some of the holes in the keel with epoxy cement. Then I put a new coat of varnish on the paddles and hung them up to dry.

In each end of the canoe was a flotation chamber so it would never sink. My father always made us tie a safety line between our belts and the canoe so that if it turned over, it couldn't be blown away from us. And of course we always wore life jackets.

My father wondered why I was working on the canoe so early in the spring, and I said that I just wanted to be ready. I didn't say what I wanted to be ready for, but remember, I didn't really know what I wanted to be ready for.

About a week before Easter, Pete's shanty disappeared. It wasn't on the shore, and we couldn't see it out on the ice. We hadn't seen Pete for nearly two weeks, and there was no doubt that his shanty had gone through the surface. I wanted to go out and see what had happened, because the ice was still strong enough, but Tracy said not to. She said that Pete had probably just forgotten about the shanty or couldn't get it off the ice in time. Anyway, the shanty was lost, and there was nothing that anyone could do about it now. She said that the ice was moving constantly, and that it was very unsafe. I wondered where Pete was, and I would have liked to see him to make sure he was all right.

One night I had a dream that he was in his shanty, and the ice broke up around him, and the whole shanty went down through the ice with him in it. In my dream I was there, too, and so was Tracy and the water was coming in around the door. And while we were trying to keep the door shut something huge and dark came tearing through it, and Tracy and Pete were swept away in the cold black water, and I woke up shaking.

Then for about a week it rained. All the snow was washed away, and the days were gray and cold. A miserable wind blew off the lake and drove the rain against us as we walked home from school one afternoon. I put my head down and pulled my yellow rain slicker up under my hat so I could hardly see where I was going. Tracy was walking backward to keep her back to the wind. That kind of wind is colder than the coldest wind of winter. After I had gone a ways I realized that she wasn't walking beside me any more. I stopped and turned around. The wind had gotten stronger, and there was cold water running down my neck. I wanted to get home as soon as I could.

Tracy was standing looking out at the lake. The lake was gray, and the rain was gray, and the clouds were gray. The rain was in my eyes, and I could barely make out the shoreline.

"What are you waiting for?" I called over the noise of the wind.

"Look!" she said, "Look at that, out there, come here quick!"

I went back and looked out in the direction she was pointing.

"What?" I said, "I don't see anything."

The rain and the water were mixed and wind was ripping the surface of the lake. I was miserably cold.

"Right there," she said.

I put my head level with her shoulder and sighted down her arm just like a rifle.

In the middle of the cove, right about where we had our shanty, in the middle of the chopped-

up waves and whitecaps, there was a small patch of what looked like perfectly calm water. There was no reason for it to be there. Not one reason in the world, at least no reason I knew of.

I raised my head and looked again. As we stood and watched, the calm area grew smaller and smaller, and vanished in the waves. I didn't feel cold any more, and I wasn't even aware of the rain stinging my face. I felt a strange light feeling, as if I weighed nothing at all.

We watched until it grew too dark, our eyes straining to see change. Then we walked home without saying a word.

Later that night, Tracy called me into her room.

"I've got to tell you what we saw today," she said. "What we saw was part of whatever is out there, and whatever has been there all winter under the ice. It's the same thing that has been there for years, and it's the same thing that has those big scales we pulled up, and it's the same thing that Pete pulled scales off years ago."

"How long has it been there?" I asked.

"I don't know," she said, "maybe hundreds of years, maybe thousands."

"But what is it? Do you know?"

She was quiet for a while.

"Do you want to know?" she said.

The next day it began to clear up, and the sun came through the clouds. The warm weather was certainly here to stay. Very little ice was left on the lake.

At the end of the week we carried the canoe down to the water's edge and put it behind an old boathouse that wasn't being used. The water was a pretty blue-gray color, and the sky was full of soft clouds. We could see the mountains on the other side of the lake plainly, and they looked as if they were very close. The sun was warm, and the air was still, really beautiful weather after the months of winter. It seemed impossible that there was anything to be worried about out in the lake. We could see the ferry from Burlington chugging across, loaded with cars and people. Some small sailboats were already out in the water.

I suggested that we take a short paddle around the cove.

"Tonight," Tracy said.

"Are you crazy?" I said. But even as I argued

with her, I knew what she had in mind. And I also knew that if she was determined to go I'd have to go along. In the first place, if there was anything there I wanted to see it. And in the second place, I couldn't let a little girl go off by herself in a canoe on a lake at night, even if she was my sister.

It was Friday night, and my parents were going off for one of their rare evenings out with some friends. They were going to a movie and then out afterwards. They wouldn't be back until about eleven, so we figured we had plenty of time. As my mother went out the door, she always said the same thing: "Be careful and don't do anything foolish." Well, at least I was going to be careful, and that was something.

It was still partially light when we left the house and walked down to where the old boathouse was.

"Whatever it is," Tracy explained, "only moves at night, and that's why no one's ever seen it."

"Why would it move at all?" I asked.

"Because," she said, "the water's gotten warmer. And that warmth will wake it up, and it will start to look around for food. It has been hibernating all winter, and it has used up its stored body fat. In order to eat it has to move."

I thought that if it was that hungry, maybe this wasn't such a good idea. Who could tell what this thing thought was a good evening meal?

We slipped the canoe down to the water's edge. I helped Tracy in, and handed her my father's big flashlight. Then I swung the stern end around for myself. She remembered to tie the safety line to a loop of her jeans.

The canoe slid out into the still water.

By this time a bright moon had come up over the mountains, and the lake surface reflected like spilled diamonds. It wasn't cold, but it wasn't warm either. Tracy had on a windbreaker and sweatshirt under it, but all I had on was my old navy sweater.

When we were about as far out from shore as my father's shanty had been we paddled around for a while trying to look down through the water. Tracy pointed the flashlight down in the water, but we couldn't see anything.

Suddenly there were some bubbles off to one side of the canoe. Tracy and I both froze.

We watched as the bubbles increased. The beam of the light made them sparkle and gleam. There was a strange smell coming with them, a smell I didn't like. It was like old garbage and paint and diesel oil and soap all mixed together.

The water moved and a large ripple rocked the canoe. An enormous bubble burst through the surface and a circle of green foam spread across

the water toward us. I put a paddle in and began to back the canoe away. There was another huge bubble and more foam.

"Let's get out of here," I said and began to swing the canoe around. Tracy was still holding the light and watching the green foam, not paying any attention to me.

"Come on!" I shouted. "Paddle or we're going to be in trouble."

But we were already in trouble, and in the next minute it was all over. Everything that I had worried about in my life before, everything that I had ever been afraid of didn't amount to anything compared to how scared I was in those next minutes.

The water rose up like a huge green mushroom, with the green foam and weeds rolling over the top. A spray covered us. The waves made a loud rushing and hissing sound; little flecks of mud fell around us.

Then out of the middle of all the bubbling and boiling water something black and solid, covered with mud and slate and weeds went up into the air above us. And as the water streamed off it and a large wave carried our canoe farther away from it, it got bigger and higher and darker. More water ran down its sides carrying away the mud and silt that covered it. It turned, and I saw that it had a face, with yellow eyes that caught the flashlight beam, and a pointed nose. I heard it struggling for breath, and water and spray ran and puffed out of its nose. It was a terrible sound, like something drowning, a high wheezing noise that was loud in my ears.

There are times in your life when you are so scared and so sure that the end is coming that you aren't really scared at all. There are times when you know that whatever happens next, you can't do anything about it, and so you might as well just be calm. We sat there in the canoe with this thing towering over us and waited for whatever was going to happen next.

What happened next was nothing. The monster stood there in the bright moonlight weaving back and forth, blinking its yellow eyes like an old man who had just come out into the sun. It didn't seem to notice us yet, and then I did a very stupid thing.

I swung the canoe around and began to paddle like a wild man. I tore at the water throwing up a furious spray.

"Stop," Tracy said, too loudly, but I paid no attention. I had the canoe under way, and I put every bit of my strength into flailing that paddle through the water. "Stop," she said again, but by that time the yellow eyes were on us, and a huge wave of water was coming after us.

It picked up the canoe front end first and sent it into the air. I heard myself scream, and I remember thinking about waking up in the next second, and finding this all a dream. But I didn't wake up. I don't know exactly what happened. I remember being under water, my lungs bursting, my nose and head full of water. I remember trying to find the surface, clawing through the water, not knowing which way was up. I remember the way my clothes and shoes stuck to me and seemed to hold me down.

And then in my panic I knew I was at the surface and in the white strange moonlight I could see the glittering water, and the high waves all around me. My lungs seemed to be full, and I was coughing and spitting up water. I remembered Tracy and tried to scream to her, but I had no breath to call.

The moon shone down on the lake and me, and nothing else.

I screamed for Tracy, and I screamed again. I struggled to keep my head above water in the silent moonlight.

I screamed again. But there was no answer. And then I realized that she was gone, and there was nothing I could do.

There's a little voice in each of us that says, "It's time to save yourself," and I was beginning to shake violently. It was a long way to shore, and even though I'm a pretty good swimmer I knew I would be lucky to make it at all. My clothes slowed me down, but they also kept me warmer. I remembered, as I pushed slowly through the water, that I hadn't tied the safety line to myself in the canoe, but that Tracy had.

When I got to the shore, I sat down on the rocks and tried to collect my thoughts. I searched the surface for the canoe, but I couldn't see a thing. I was still scared, and so cold that I couldn't think

clearly. My teeth were chattering and my arms and legs shook with convulsions. I stood up on the rock and called once more for Tracy even though I knew it was too late. There was only the surface of the lake and the moon and me, and Tracy was gone. And I felt so bad and so hopeless that I began to cry. I crawled up the bank to the road, slipping and falling on the rocks, cutting my ankles and my hands, but not caring at all.

The first car that came along was my parents on their way home from the movies.

The police and the neighbors searched the shore and the lake for quite a ways out, but they found nothing. Tracy and the canoe had disappeared completely. They asked me over and over what happened, but I couldn't tell them.

You have to understand that my mother was just about beside herself. She cried an awful lot, and I thought she was going to lose her mind from sadness. My father was more bewildered than anything else. And in the middle of all this I couldn't tell a crazy story about a monster. In the first place, nobody would believe me, and in the second place they would think that I was making up lies about something that was very sad. So I had the truth all to myself, and it wasn't much comfort.

In fact, I couldn't figure out what had happened myself. Where had Tracy disappeared to, and what had happened to the canoe? There were no answers.

I tried to make up some story to explain why

we were out in the lake that night, but nothing I could say made much sense. After a while my parents stopped asking me. They told me they were just grateful I was alive, but I knew that they still wondered what had really happened.

I stayed home from school for a week until I felt better. I really didn't want to go back to school at all, because I knew everybody would be asking questions. But when I finally did go back, everybody was very nice. No one talked about what had happened. They just said they were very sorry about Tracy.

I was having a hard time paying attention to school anyway. The thoughts of what happened that night kept going through my head. And whenever I began to think of it, I would feel the cold water and weeds and muck on me and hear my voice screaming for Tracy.

The third day I was back at school someone brought a message that my grandfather was in the office and wanted to see me. My grandfather lives in Boston and never comes up to see us, so I knew it had to be somebody else.

It was Pete. He stood up when I came into the office and made a quick motion to me to be quiet. In three seconds he had scooted me out the door

and into his old truck. He looked scared and very tired. His clothes were filthy and his boots were caked with mud and slime. As we drove down the driveway of the school, I could hear somebody shouting after us. It hadn't taken them long to figure out that Pete wasn't really anybody's grandfather, certainly not mine.

Pete didn't talk much. On the front seat of the truck were groceries, mostly canned goods. In the bed I could see cans of gasoline and two-cycle oil.

I hadn't seen Pete since the winter, but he was acting so strangely that I wasn't sure about any conversation.

"You gotta promise to never say anything about this, boy," he said at last. "Never say nothing to nobody."

"But where are we going?" I asked.

"Nothing to nobody, you understand?" he said, checking the rear-view mirror nervously.

"OK," I said, because I could see I wasn't going to learn anything until I agreed. He kept looking back to see if anyone was following us but nobody was.

But even then he didn't say anything. We drove along a road that led to a small cape that sticks out in the lake. At the very end, Pete's boat was tied behind some trees at the water's edge.

58

Pete told me to load up the boat and bail out some of the water. He was in a terrible hurry. As he mixed the fuel he rushed and spilled half of it on the ground. His hands were shaking as he poured it into the outboard tank, and it ran down the floor of the boat.

Pete's outboard was even older than his boat and in worse shape. By the time he got it started,

60

it was late afternoon. He kept looking up to see if any cars were coming down the road, and he got madder and madder at the motor.

When it finally started I still knew no more

about where we were going than I had before. We seemed to be well prepared for a long trip. There was a great deal of food, but no fishing gear. We had three extra gasoline cans, each holding five gallons. That was enough to go a long way. Packed in with everything else was a large clear plastic bag of clothes. As I looked at the bag I realized that they were Tracy's clothes. Sure enough, packed in that bag was the green sweater that my mother had knitted for Tracy for Christmas. And there were her boots and even the little plastic camera that I had given her.

I was getting very scared, partly because Pete was acting so strange, and partly because it was getting so late. I was about to ask Pete why Tracy's clothes were there and where we were going and if I couldn't just go home now, when the motor finally came to life. It sputtered and coughed, and the boat turned and nosed into the lake.

Pete didn't relax until we were about a mile out in the middle. It's not very safe out in the middle in a small motor boat, and the waves threw it from side to side. But I knew that Pete wanted to be far enough so we couldn't be clearly seen. As the sun began to fade he drew back closer to the shore.

"Now," he said, "get some food out for me, open a can of something. I'm starving."

I opened a can of pork and beans, and he ate them cold with his jackknife.

We went north for what seemed to be hours. The mountains that are on each side of the lake were behind us. The coastline was now flat, and we were in the islands at the northern end of the lake. We went under the bridge at Rouses Point, and I knew we were close to the Canadian border. By this time it was dark, and the few cars on the bridge had their headlights on. They wouldn't have been able to see anything of us.

Pete stopped to put more gasoline in the tank. He rummaged around in the groceries and got out some bread and a jar of jelly. He made us some sandwiches and poured some hot chocolate from a thermos.

And then he began to talk.

"I hope I didn't scare you too much," he said, much calmer and more like his old self, "but I was so afraid of getting caught, and I didn't want you to know anything if we did get caught. We're pretty close to Canada now and once I take you across the border I can get in real trouble."

He took another long drink of the hot chocolate and began to make another sandwich. The moonlight was still very bright. The water glittered to the south, and the bridge lights ran off to the west. A chilly wind made me pull my sweater close about me.

"About this time in the evening," Pete continued, "when all boys and girls should be home in bed, about ten days ago, I was coming ashore in this very boat after a day fishing. I saw somebody with a light out in a canoe looking for something in the water." He paused, "Who do you think it was?"

I didn't answer. He went on.

"And as they was looking for whatever it was, whatever it was showed up. Only it was a lot bigger and scarier than they bargained for. And they tried to get out of the way, but they weren't fast enough."

He ate for a while, and what he was saying sunk into my head. I remembered the feel of the cold water and my lungs bursting.

"And their little canoe turned over, and they

66

got thrown out into the cold water. And then I
heard one of them screaming, and I recognized a
name. And that whatever-it-was was awful big,
and it came thrashing through the water like a
destroyer, right at me with all sorts of stuff stuck
on it. I recognized my old shanty on its back, the
one that went through the ice. And there were
68

weeds and branches and parts of old rowboats and
rope and everything. My shanty was hanging on
for dear life, and I figured I might be able to get it
back. The waves nearly turned me over, but I was
able to turn the prow into the worst waves and
ride over them. The thing moved off into deeper
water and veered to the north. And then I heard

another voice calling, a higher voice. And I said to myself, 'Pete,' I said, 'you know that voice, don't you?' "

Pete ate some more. I sat and waited, feeling like I was floating on air.

"So I followed it north," he continued. "It went faster than this old boat could keep up, but it left a wake, just like a ferry. I followed the wake and the trail of junk that had fallen off all the way up here into these marshes. But then it was dark and pretty gloomy as you can see. I was running low on gas, and I had very little food with me. I nosed around in the swamp islands for a while, and then I stopped and listened. And you know what I heard?"

Pete stopped and looked at me and smiled for the first time since we had left the school.

"I heard somebody crying, and it sounded like a little girl."

By this time we had drifted closer to a large island covered with thick swamp grass. There was still some light in the sky to the south. The water was calm and a slight breeze rustled through the grass. Pete was still looking right at me.

"And do you know what I did?" he asked.

I couldn't answer.

"Well," he said, "I hollered out. Like this."
Pete put his hands to his mouth and called.
"TRA—CEE!"

We sat and waited in the boat, and the nicest little sound came back from the black shadows of the marshes. I could barely hear it, but I recogniz-ed the voice. And all the sadness and hopelessness of the past week rolled off my back and disappeared into the lake.

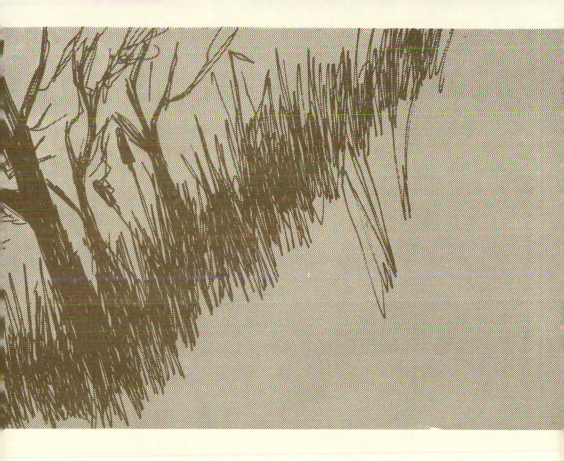

Pete started the motor and we went to the voice. We went deep into the tall marsh grass and down a little curving river that wandered into the darkness. I strained my eyes to see a sign of anything. And then I saw a little fire flickering against a black hill in the middle of the marsh. And sitting by the fire was my sister.

It's funny to think about her being alive all that time. All that time when we thought she was dead. But even then she was only alive for me and Pete. To my parents she was still gone forever. Forever, except it would not be forever, even though they didn't know it.

We pulled the boat up, and Tracy hugged Pete and then me, and we were sure glad to see each other. I gave her some candy. Pete boiled some water and made us all chicken noodle soup.

We sat and talked, and I told her all about Mom and Dad and what they thought had happened. I told her about how I couldn't tell them what really happened, because no one would believe me and would probably think I was crazy.

"Well, you weren't crazy," she said. "But it's a good thing you didn't say anything. Look!"

A little way from the fire stood Pete's fishing shanty sunk at a slight angle in the grass, still covered with mud and weeds. But in the dark it almost looked kind of homey. Everything had been lost out of it when it sunk, but it was still sound enough to protect Tracy from the weather.

I had been so glad to see her and so happy to find her alive that I hadn't asked her about what happened. It seemed that no one was exactly rushing to tell me either.

"You must promise to do what I ask," she said when she saw the question in my eyes. "You must keep the secret and promise to help."

Here I was, out in the dark swamps, north of the Canadian border with my sister who had just come back from the dead, and an old man who had saved her, and I had to promise to keep a secret before I was even told. So I promised.

What we had seen come up out of the lake, what had turned over our canoe and had carried Tracy way up north, what Pete had followed for miles in his boat was something that had been living in the lake since even before there were men on the shore. It was big and old, and it had hidden for centuries beneath the surface, coming out at night and spending most of the summer in swamps and bogs where motor boats and fishermen never go. In the winter it ventured down the middle of the lake where it could find deeper waters to hibernate in. It had survived because of its shyness and because it was good at hiding. It had probably been seen by people before, but people who said they had seen a monster in the lake were thought to be crazy.

Tracy had been tied in the canoe when the monster surfaced. The line on the prow of the canoe fell overboard and got tangled in the junk and weeds that had collected on the back of the monster. For part of the time she had been underwater. But the canoe had been upside down over her and there was enough trapped air for her to breathe. Then the canoe had rolled out from under branches, or the branches had fallen away, and she had miraculously wound up sitting upright in the canoe half way down the monster's back. She had a chance to gather her wits and get over her fear.

She also had a chance to look at the monster.
And the first thing she noticed was that it was
very, very old. There were large wrinkles around
its head, and the skin hung in loose folds. Several
times it turned around and looked at her on its
back, and she was sure that it was going to knock
her off into the cold water. But it didn't seem to
see her clearly. One of its eyes seemed to be blind
and was partially closed, and most of its teeth

were missing. Its head hung almost down to the water line.

The farther north they went the slower the monster swam, until it was just barely moving when it got to the swamps. Tracy was so cold that she nearly passed out. She shivered and tried to scrunch down in the canoe to stay out of the wind.

The moon was high in the sky, and she could see the swamp islands stretching out to either side of the river.

The monster had come to a stop. It was lying over a little island with part of its long body still in the water. Tracy could hear it breathing very slowly, making a strange sound, wheezing and struggling every time it inhaled. Its back rose and fell slowly.

She got up a little out of the canoe and tried to see the head, but it was buried in the dark weeds. A large branch was stuck to the monster's back and reached down to the ground. She could get out and somehow climb down. But just as she started to lean over for the branch, the monster gave a huge moan and rolled over. Tracy lost her balance. The branch fell away. Pete's shanty tumbled past her, and she fell into the soft swamp grass with the shanty landing in a soggy lump beside her.

The monster was still breathing heavily. It was a sad sort of sound now. And Tracy was sad enough for the both of them. She was cold and tired and hungry. She didn't know where she was, but she was sure there was no way out. She couldn't get the canoe and the paddles were lost anyway. She sat in the moonlight and cried.

Then she thought her ears were playing tricks on her. She thought that the cold had gotten into

her head and that the angels were coming for her. She thought that she heard a voice calling her name. It called again and again. Suddenly she realized that someone was there. She struggled through the dark grass and called back.

Within fifteen minutes Pete had her wrapped in his jacket and had started a small fire of dry grass. She slept that night in Pete's jacket with his boat cushion for a pillow, and Pete stayed up to keep the fire going.

"It was Pete who wanted to get you," Tracy said, "so we'd have at least one other witness later on."

"But why?" I asked, "Why not tell Mom and Dad right away?"

"Well, I was out of gas for one thing," Pete said. "I had to row for three days till I found a road. I knew I could get you out here without making a full explanation. But I'd have to tell the entire story to your folks before they'd come. And what if they didn't believe me? They'd think I was a crazy old man, and your ma's been through enough grief."

"So," Tracy said, "we decided to snatch you and bring you up here. And swear you to secrecy."

That was the story Tracy told me as we sat out there in the marshes, she and Pete and I around a little flickering fire. It was the most amazing story I had ever heard, but there was one question I still had. And just as I started to ask it I looked up and saw the answer and my blood froze. A chill ran down my back and my jaw dropped.

The black hill that rose in the center of the island not fifty feet from where we were sitting was no hill at all. It was the answer to my question, "Where is the monster now?" I started up, but Tracy saw my fear. She looked at Pete, and he laughed quietly.

"I wondered when you'd realize it was there," she said.

"You mean that's it, right there?" I looked at the long, dark shape.

"Eddie," she said, "there's nothing to be afraid of. It can't hurt you, and it wouldn't even if it could. It's dying, Eddie, it may be dead already.

It's very old, maybe thousands of years, and all it wants is to be able to die in peace. It's a peaceful **animal, and it should be able to die as it wants to.**"

By the next morning the monster was definitely no longer alive. Tracy gave me a full tour while Pete worked on his outboard. She showed me where the scales had been pulled off by fishing hooks, where old scars had healed in its sides, where cans and trash from the bottom of the lake had become lodged in its skin, where mud and slime had coated its back and where weeds and other plants had taken root.

In the sunlight, the monster was enormous; its green scales drying up like old shingles where they were out of the water.

I felt sorry now that it was dead. It looked very old and wrinkled, and I wondered what kind of a life it had had. I asked Tracy why we had to keep it a secret now if it was dead.

"Because you promised, that's why," she said, "but that's not the only reason."

She led me to the island's edge where the monster's tail disappeared into the water. The water was clear up here in the marshes, not cloudy as it is in the lake.

In the shallow water was the reason for Tracy's secrecy. It was round and green and kind of transparent, with lighter markings in parallel rings. In the sunlight it looked like a gigantic green pearl.

It had a strange rubbery feel to it when we loaded it into the canoe. Tracy put some fresh marsh grass around it to cushion it, and it looked just like an Easter egg in a basket.

We tied the canoe to the outboard and broke camp. Pete and I cleaned up as much as we could. Then the three of us went to work covering the monster with grass and branches. It took a long

time but Tracy was determined that the carcass wouldn't be spotted from the air. By the middle of the afternoon, we were through, and Pete started the motor. We headed out into the channel and pretty soon the bridge was in sight.

Well, needless to say, my parents were very happy to see us back. My mother says her life has started all over again. Old Pete is quite the hero around our house, and we go fishing together, the three of us.

The only time we talk about what happened is when we're out in the boat alone. And then only when we're pretty far from shore.

Since I'm sworn to secrecy, I can't tell you what Tracy did with the egg. I'm not even supposed to tell whether it hatched or not, and I've probably told too much already.

But a secret is hard to keep. I sometimes wish that I didn't know about the monster and the egg. I'm sure people would think I was crazy if I did talk about it. But if I don't talk about it, I'll forget it, and I don't want to forget it. I guess that's why I'm writing it down.

Tracy doesn't know I'm writing all this down. She'd probably say I've broken my promise. But I haven't really.

Maybe someday, when I'm real old, say eighteen or nineteen, I'll make this into a book. Maybe Tracy will have forgotten my promise by then, or won't care.

Besides, even if I did write it in a book, no one would believe it anyway.

I mean, you don't believe it, do you?